To Our Young Readers:

As dogs and wild beasts usually don't mix well, what does a little girl who lives on a Nature Conservancy in Kenya do since she is not allowed to have a dog? Of course: She takes in a pet rhinoceros.

When we first saw Peter Greste's stunning photographs of a lovable young rhino named Lola and the blond-haired Tiva frolicking in the mud together, we were mesmerized at the story line suggested by the photos. Lola and Tiva's story almost doesn't need words: a blind mother rhino can't keep track of her offspring once they begin to walk more than a few steps; her still-nursing baby, Lola, wanders off one day and gets lost, and finally she meets a family with a caring young daughter who takes Lola in as an unusual but quite suitable substitute for the dog she can't have.

Lola and Tiva is the living metaphor of every young animal lover's dream: to feed, take care of, keep company, and yes, even roll around in the mud with a wild beast who you then put to bed at night and tuck in with their favorite blanket. We hope you enjoy the magically true story of Lola and Tiva.

With hope and peace,
Craig, Juliana, and Isabella Hatkoff

137685 EN
Lola & Tiva: An Unlikely Friendship

Hatkoff, Juliana
ATOS BL 3.3
Points: 0.5   LG

Text copyright © 2010 by Turtle Pond Publications LLC

All rights reserved. Published by Scholastic Inc.
SCHOLASTIC, CARTWHEEL BOOKS,
and associated logos are trademarks
and/or registered trademarks of Scholastic Inc.
Lexile is a registered trademark of MetaMetrics, Inc.

ISBN 978-0-545-20728-7
10 9 8 7 6 5 4 3 2 1   10 11 12 13 14 15/0

Printed in the U.S.A.
First printing, January 2010   40

LEVEL 2 SCHOLASTIC READER 250-750 WORDS

Lola & Tiva

An Unlikely Friendship

Told by

JULIANA, ISABELLA, *and* CRAIG HATKOFF

Photos by Peter Greste

Cartwheel BOOKS®

SCHOLASTIC INC.

New York Toronto London Auckland

Sydney Mexico City New Delhi Hong Kong

There is a very special place in Kenya, Africa, called the Lewa Wildlife Conservancy. Lewa is a large place where animals roam free, and people – called rangers – watch over them. A young girl named Tiva lived there with her family. Her father worked for Lewa.

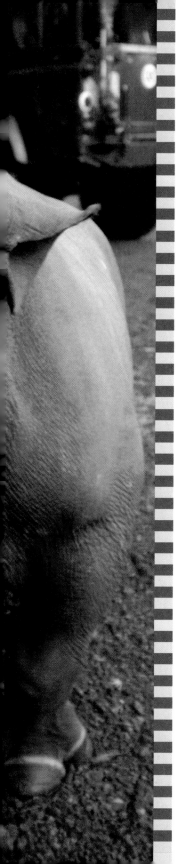

Everyone at Lewa knew that Tiva had always wanted a puppy. But puppies were not allowed. Instead the people at Lewa found Tiva a different kind of friend— a young black rhino named Lola. Lola seemed to work just as well as a puppy for Tiva. Lola and Tiva became the best of friends. This is their true story.

Lola was born at Lewa to a mother that was blind. For a couple of days Lola drank her mother's milk for food and stayed close by. But when she was strong enough to walk, Lola wandered off to another area of Lewa. Her mother could not see Lola walking away. Without her mother to feed and protect her, Lola was in danger.

Lola needed food and could become a meal for a lion or another hungry animal. She could not find her mother and her blind mother could not find her. The rangers who worked at Lewa searched for Lola. When they found her, they brought her to a safe place in Lewa that was near Tiva's house. There, Lola would be out of danger.

Tiva was excited when
Lola arrived. She wanted
to take care of Lola.
Like any baby, Lola
needed many things.
Most of all, Lola was
hungry and needed milk.
Tiva learned to feed Lola.
Lola drank a bottle five
times a day. Each time,
she drank over a gallon!

Tiva loved Lola. Lola was a lot like a big puppy.

She tried to climb things. She licked things. She smelled things.

She begged at the dinner table.

Like most pets, Lola never posed when Tiva tried to take pictures. She wanted to nap.

But Lola did like for Tiva to pet her
between the ears.

Of course, rhinos are not really
like dogs. They don't eat dog food.
When Lola was about five months
old, she started to eat like a real rhino.
She ate shrubs, twigs, and leaves. Her
upper lip is shaped like a hook and
can grab onto food. Lola could wrap
her hook around sticks and leaves. But
she still loved to drink her milk, too.

Rhinos in the wild are usually shy. They often run away if they see or smell people. Lola was too young to be afraid of people. Tiva and the rangers became her family.

A baby rhino is called a calf. A calf usually stays with its mother for two years. The mother watches over her calf. Lola needed someone to look after her. Tiva became Lola's special friend.

Like a pet, Lola needed special care.
Tiva helped pick bugs off Lola's body.
The bugs could make Lola sick.
In the wild, birds eat the bugs off a
rhino's skin. But birds would not do
that for Lola. There were too many
people around.

Lola also needed to take baths. Mud baths! When a rhino rolls in the mud, it is called wallowing. It is an important part of being a rhino.
The mud protects a rhino's skin from the sun – like sunscreen. Once the mud dries, it also keeps bugs from biting.

Tiva made sure Lola knew how to wallow. It isn't as easy as it looks. It takes a lot of practice.
A rhino does not have to wash the mud off. A little girl does.

Lola and Tiva shared
their days together.
Lola learned about being
a rhinoceros. Tiva learned
about being a friend.
It was a lot of fun, and it
wore them out.